Diary of a Farting Creeper

Book 2

How Does the Creeper

<u>DOUBLE</u>

His Power?

-Wimpy Fart-

This book is unofficial and unauthorized. It is not authorized, approved, licensed, or endorsed by Mojang.

You're awesome for reading

Wimpy Fart Books!

Thank You!

Table of Contents

Tuesday

Last week, a bunch of events completely changed my life! Before last week, I was the biggest joke in school because, instead of exploding like other creepers, I fart! But now everyone recognizes the power of my farts. Instead of Wimpy the farting creeper, I'm Wimpy the super-creeper!

All of those creepers who used to bully me and call me names in school want to be my friend, and they want me to teach them how to fart. In just a couple of days the world around me completely changed.

My parents are a lot happier now, probably because I'm happier and I smile and talk a lot more now. Addison and I are friends now, too.

It's amazing! She just came to me one day and said she wanted to be friends. At first my response was, "You want to be friends now? You never said anything about it when I was just a farting creeper and everyone else was making fun of me."

"Well, I'm not like everyone else. If you think about it, you'll remember that I was never one of the ones who called you names or anything like that."

"Well, that's true."

"The only reason I never spoke to you before or tried to be your friend is that I thought you weren't interested in talking to others or making friends. You don't hang out with us on Sundays, you never come to the movies, and you never really talk to anyone, so I thought you just wanted to keep to yourself."

"Well, what made you change your mind, and why are you talking to me now?"

"Someone who can scare dogs and cats the way you do is really cool!" She smiled.

"OK, Addison," I grinned back at her, "maybe one day I'll show you how to scare cats."

That's how Addison and I became friends.

"Do you want to hang out after school tomorrow?" she asked.

"Tomorrow I'm meeting up with my friend Steve the skeleton.

"What about Thursday?"

"Right now, I don't have any plans on Thursday, but I might be busy. So, it's better to plan something for another day."

"Okay. My parents want to meet you. They're different, too, and they've always liked you," Addison said.

"Your parents know me? That's strange. How do they know who I am? Is it because of my farts?"

"My dad is the gym teacher and the soccer coach, he likes you a lot. He keeps saying that you're one of his favorites because you always listen and you're a team player."

I was really surprised to hear that. But then I remembered that Coach has always treated me like a regular creeper, which is why I have so much fun playing soccer. He never talked about my farts or made fun of me. While the other creepers were fooling around and making jokes, I was always practicing soccer drills so that I could get better and better. Now that I know Addison is Coach's daughter, we're definitely going to be friends.

Wednesday

Creepers at school keep coming up to me and try to be friends. I decided to stay away from most of them because they say they want to be friends now and hang out, but I still remember the days when they used to bully me and call me names.

One creeper cornered me in the bathroom at school and asked me to teach him how to fart. I just wanted to get back to class, so I told him first he has to sit on the toilet. When he sat down and closed the door, I waited a few seconds. Then I farted really loud.

BBBRRRRRRRZZZTHHHPPPPTTT

The sound shook the bathroom and I heard him fall in the toilet water. He actually started crying!

Don't get me wrong. I'm happy everyone wants to be friends now, and there's no point being angry about the past, but I'm not going to teach them how to fart. I don't need to be friends with them, I'll stick to hanging out with my skeleton and zombie friends, Steve and LJ. At least I know Steve and LJ are my real friends and they liked me even before my fart power came to good use.

Most of these other creepers are friends with anyone they think can benefit them. I don't play those games; I'd rather make real friends.

Thursday

I had a lot to do today, but before I got out of bed I wanted to practice some farts under the blanket.

BBBBRRRRRRRZZZTHHHPPPPTTT

I practiced for over an hour. Now my room smells like fart, and I can't use that blanket anymore. Then I went to meet up with Steve and LJ.

Even though I know where the zombies and skeletons from Steve and LJ's clan live, we decided to meet in the woods.

"Hey Steve!!"

"Hi, it's good to see you again."

"Hi LJ...How are you doing?"

"I'm better than ever," he said.

"Do you want to talk about the plan here, or should we go underground?" I asked.

"This place is fine," Steve replied. "But tomorrow we'll have to go underground and meet the doctor."

"Why? Does he want to give me more tests?"

"No, no. All the tests are done. Now, he just wants to give you a strict diet plan to follow. This way, your farts will be even more powerful."

"I think my farts are strong enough. I scared the wolves, remember? And I can shake the bathroom at school."

"We know, but the doctor believes that as you grow older, your body won't be able to produce those gases as easily. Ender's diet plan will help you produce those gases whenever you want to, through the rest of your life."

"That would definitely be a great thing for me."

"Not just for you, but for all the mobs."

"You're more valuable than any other creeper around," LJ said.

"Do you really think so? I'd be lying if I said that I am not proud of what I've done or could do for you. But I don't think I am that powerful."

"Of course, you will have to keep your farts to make them more powerful, and the doctor's advice will help you with that. But even at this stage it's clear that you're a Super Creeper."

"Oh, wow. I went from Stink Bomb to Super Creeper. Awesome!"

Steve laughed. "Our Ender told us that creepers' weak point is that they disappear when they explode, and you don't have that weak point because you don't explode. Now, if you work to make your farts more powerful, you'll automatically become the strongest creeper in history."

"Hmm, I kind of like that idea."

"Let's get to the point now," Steve said. "The humans are again planning big attacks. Actually, they are planning a series of attacks."

"Will they be back-to-back attacks?" I asked.

"We don't know their exact plans yet. The spiders only told us that the humans won't be bringing cats and dogs this time. And instead of tamed wolves, they are probably bringing wild ones."

"How will they bring wild wolves without taming them? They're just normal humans and the wild wolves will eat them."

"Wolves don't usually attack humans unless they're really hungry. If they're only a little hungry the humans are safe, but we're not, so we need to figure out how to fight off the wolves."

"I scared some wolves before with my fart, but if these wolves are wild then will that be enough?" I asked.

"We'll just have to see. I think you can scare them if your farts are loud enough, because wolves have really strong ears, stronger than dogs. But we'll need to have a plan."

"How much time do we have?"

"They won't be attacking us before next weekend."

"Why do the humans only attack on weekends?" I was really curious to know.

"They're like us; they have to go to school or work during the week so their only free time is on Saturdays and Sundays."

"Are they imitating us?"

"I think so."

I need to figure out how to double my fart power before the attack. Hopefully the doctor can help me. Then I can fight off the wolves, and the humans too.

Friday

I met up with Steve and LJ again. I wanted to invite them over for dinner so they can see my room. They were surprised I invited them over. They started saying I'm more confident now and they want to be like me. At first, I thought they were just making fun of me, because creepers at school used to say stuff like that. They would tell me I'm good at something but then it turns out they were actually making fun of me.

I asked Steve and LJ if they were serious.

"Yes, really," LJ said. "You fought for creatures you didn't even know a few days ago, and it has changed. Now you're not afraid of anything. "

"I agree," Steve said.

"I'm glad you're different now. You remind me of my cousin MJ. MJ is a mini zombie, he used to get bullied a lot, but then he learned how to fight and now he's one of the most popular mini zombies ever." LJ said.

"So do you guys want to come over for dinner next week?"

"Are you sure it's okay? Do your parents know everything now?" LJ asked.

"They know that I am helping you fight off the humans, but they don't know anything about our plans, or where we meet, or that we talk to the spider because the spiders are spying on the humans for us."

"I think we should get the diet from the doctor first. Then you guys can come over and we can keep working on a plan."

"Alright! Can you save some zombie food for me?" LJ asked.

"What do you mean?"

"Zombies only eat rotten food and garbage. So ask your mom not to throw away the trash and I'll eat it when we come over." LJ said.

"I can't ask my mom to save the garbage, can you please eat normal food?"

"Okay. But I can't tell my parents or I'll get in trouble. Zombies are supposed to eat like zombies, if they find out I tried normal food I might get grounded".

"Steve, how about you? I think you eat everything that we eat right?"

"I'm a skeleton, food just falls on the floor when I eat so I don't really care" Steve said.

So now we're all set. I'll ask mom to make something for us to eat, and when Steve and LJ come over we can talk more about how to fight off the wolves. I'm going to do some research on wolves at home. Once school starts on Monday, I'll have access to some more books. I'll check them for information, too.

I have to meet Steve and LJ near the Ender's place on Monday. Hopefully he can double my farts, then I'll be unstoppable! I keep trying to push my farts harder but I'm afraid I'll explode, so I'll wait to see what the doctor wants me to do.

Saturday

I told Mom that I invited Steve and LJ over for dinner next week. She said they can't go in my room because it still smells like farts.

"This is the first time you invited your friends over, I don't want them to get sick because of your smelly farts!"

"But, Mom, Steve is a Skeleton so I don't think he can smell anything, and LJ is a Zombie. Zombies don't brush their teeth and they never take a bath, so I think we'll be okay."

"Fine. What do you want to eat, I can cook anything" mom said.

"Anything. Steve doesn't care and LJ is going to eat whatever you cook."

"Alright, I'll figure it out. Don't worry, just have fun with your friends and try not to fart while they're in your room."

Dad must have heard me talking to Mom, because he walked in and asked what we were talking about. When we told him that I invited my friends for dinner, he, too, seemed happy.

I told them I was going to see the doctor Monday after school. They got concerned and started asking questions, I think they're afraid the doctor will fix me and I'll be able to explode.

I told them the doctor just wants to make me more powerful. Mom asked me to take notes so that I can tell her what the doctor told me when I get home.

I started reading more books on wolves. The only useful fact I found is that they are a danger to the skeletons, but not for the zombies or other mobs in the underground village.

Sunday

I ran into LJ and his cousin MJ, the mini zombie. MJ is small but he knows how to fight. He used to get bullied just like me, but now the bigger zombies are afraid of him.

MJ wanted to show me some moves, so he asked if he could kick me. LJ reminded him that I'm a creeper and creepers explode. He doesn't know I 'm different and I fart instead, but I didn't say anything. I'm glad LJ distracted him; otherwise I would have farted in his mini zombie face!

Steve showed up. I told him wolves don't like skeletons, but they're ok with zombies. LJ is pretty excited, but Steve is scared now.

"So, what do you think we should do?" LJ asked.

"I think I should teach Steve and some other skeletons how to fart. This way they can help me fight off the wolves. Then you and the zombies can fight with the humans face-to-face."

"It's an interesting plan," Steve said.

LJ liked my plan too, but he wasn't 100% sure.

"I think the zombies will be ok with the plan, but do you really think you can teach skeletons how to fart," he said.

I told them I did some research on the internet once and I was looking for pictures of farts but I kept finding pictures of humans and skeletons.

"Steve, is that true?" LJ asked .

Steve knew about this. He said, "Yea it's true, skeletons can fart, but our farts are small and quiet. We can probably teach the young skeletons in our village how to fart, but like I said, they're not too powerful so we'll need loudspeakers there to maximize their sound."

So now we have a basic plan now. After the doctor tomorrow I'll have more info, hopefully I can use it to help the younger skeletons fart too.

Monday

We met up at the doctor's office after school. Steve rang the bell, and the doctor opened the door almost instantly.

"You are late by two minutes!"

"We're sorry, Doctor. We got lost." Steve said.

"Is he always so punctual?" I whispered to LJ as Steve was speaking to the Ender.

"Yea, that's the only problem with him. Two minutes feels like five hours for him."

"So, what will we have to do to make up for it?"

"Nothing, but he will keep talking about it all through the meeting. He can make you feel irritated at times."

"You two don't seem to have used those two minutes well," The doctor said, looking at LJ and me. "If you have more important things to discuss with each other, come back and see me in a few days." He was beginning to sound like the principal at school.

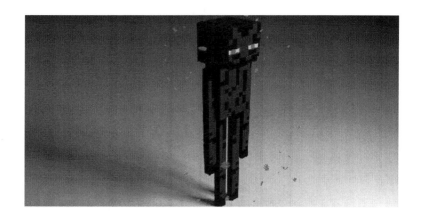

"We're sorry, Doctor. Can you please explain what you want me to do with my diet."

"Right. Your diet! I'm going to include certain things in your diet that only humans eat. The dietary habits of humans cause almost all of them to fart. Your talent gives you the ability to create loud and smelly farts, but you'll need to maximize the supply of gases. This is important since you now plan on using your farts as weapons. You will need to have a huge gas reserve to fart at will."

"Okay." I still didn' doctor was planning to do with my diet.

"Now tell me, what types of food do you love to eat?"

"Regular food, like pizza and pasta, I eat chicken and sometimes I eat hot dogs, tacos, and ice cream."

"Do you eat vegetables?"

"No way. Unless my mom makes me. Sometimes she makes salad but I just eat the salad dressing."

"You need to eat Kale for breakfast. It can easily double your fart power in just one meal. Eat it twice every day for a month before the fight. Actually, since we are just a few days away from the fight, I recommend that you eat it three times per day. But breakfast is the most import"

"Kale? I think that's what my mom puts in her morning smoothie." Is there a special way to cook it?"

"No, I think your mother should decide that. All moms eat kale. That's why Moms are the best farters in society, they just hide it really well. Kale is a super vegetables and will give you super fart power."

I never tried kale before, but I always hear my mom and her friends talk about it being good for the digestive system. I wonder if my mom really farts.

"How much do I need to eat?"

"Doesn't matter. Eat as much as you want. Just make sure you stick to dark green kale, especially for breakfast."

"Sounds good. Do you have any other special tips for him?" Steve asked the doctor.

"Just one thing: be careful if you have pets. Animals can't eat kale, it's too rough for them. No kale for animals."

"Thanks a lot, Doctor. You don't know how much you have helped us!"

LJ and I looked at each other, and I knew both of us had the same thing on our minds.

We're going to feed kale to the wolves! If they're hungry, we can feed them kale when they come after us. I don't know what will happen, but if the doctor said it's dangerous for animals then that should stop them.

Tuesday

I asked my mom if she farts and she got upset. Then I asked her what she puts in her breakfast smoothie and she got suspicious so I stopped talking. She started asking me questions about why I'm so interested, then she said only human moms fart and she warned me not to ask those question again.

Steve and LJ came over for dinner today, I introduced them to Mom and Dad. Dad said Steve is cool because he's a skeleton and Mom likes LJ because he's polite, for a Zombie.

Mom made some smoothies for us. But I don't think they had kale. Just fruit and stuff.

LJ brought a rotten banana with him and he put it inside the smoothie when Mom wasn't looking. He finished half the glass before Mom even turned around, then he told her it was delicious and he gulped the rest.

Steve and I hadn't even picked up our glasses and LJ already finished his.

We were hanging out in my room and Mom kept coming back trying to give us more food. I guess she thought we were hungry. I told Mom we had a lot to talk about so we would eat dinner later.

Steve asked if I told my mom what the doctor said about Kale.

"No, but I asked her if she farts and I asked about her morning smoothie and she got upset. So I think it might be true. What do you think?"

"You should talk to her as soon as possible. If Kale is really that powerful then we need to feed it to wolves. Ask her if she ever heard of animals eating kale." Steve said.

"Are you ready for dinner?" Mom started shouting from the kitchen.

LJ was the first one to the table again. I didn't know Zombies were always so hungry.

Dinner was pretty good. Mom had a lot of options for us to eat, but we couldn't finish it all.

Mom packed all the leftovers for LJ. He told me he would keep them in his lunch box until they start to smell and then he'll eat them, in about a week.

Wednesday

Before school today I talked to talk to Mom about eating Kale.

"Mom, yesterday I didn't get time to tell you about the Ender's diet plan for me."

"Yes, I was wondering about that. Can you show me the notes?"

I handed over the note to Mom. All it said was eat kale 3 times per day to make JUMBO farts."

"Is this why you asked me questions about my breakfast smoothie?"

"Yes, so is it true? Does Kale make you fart too?"

"I told you not to ask me that?!" She said.

I asked Mom if she ever heard of animals eating kale and she told me one of the neighbors accidentally put kale in the garbage. Their dog got into the trash can at night and the next day they had to take him to the vet.

She said the dog's stomach filled up with too much gas and he looked like a balloon.

Today is Wednesday so we had gym class. I saw both Addison again, we're in the same class. She asked me to hang out tomorrow after school. I told her I'm training to make bigger farts, so that I can scare wolves, and I have to eat kale at least 3 times per day.

"I think my mom has Kale." Addison said. Of course her mom has kale. I think the doctor was telling the truth, all Moms are fart experts!

Addison called her mom and told her I was coming over tomorrow. She asked her mom if they have kale at home. I told her to ask her mom if she farts, but her mom hung up the phone before Addison could ask.

Thursday

When school was finally over, I met up with Addison and her Dad, and the three of us walked towards the eastern part of the jungle. Addison's Mom was waiting for us at the door.

Her mom is really nice, she said she heard a lot about me. She was making green smoothies with kale because she heard I'm training my farts.

I asked her why Mom's always eat kale. Then all of a sudden my phone rang, and it was Steve.

He said the spiders uncovered some serious info.

"Should I meet you?"

"I don't think that's necessary, as long as you can talk right now I can tell you everything."

"Okay, what's up?"

"Someone from our village is sending secret information to the humans."

"You mean the humans are spying on us? Does this mean that the humans already know about our plan to feed kale to the wolves?"

"One of our own mobs is playing the role of secret agent for the humans. The good news is that, so far, the humans have no idea about our plans."

"Well, if the spy is from the village, he or she would know how we won the last battle. That is enough to increase the confidence of the humans. They won't feel threatened by my farts anymore."

"You're right. It might sound surprising, but the spy only knows that you are helping us. That person has no idea about HOW you are helping us. Our spiders are pretty sure of this information."

"I need to think about this for a bit. We have to find a solution to this problem as early as possible. Starting tomorrow, I'll be spending a lot of time in your village. If we don't identify the spy before that, we could be in deep trouble."

I ended the call, but the news had spoiled my mood completely.

"You don't look happy. Is there a big problem?" Addison asked.

"One of our own citizens is trying to spoil our plan. That person is working for the humans and is spying on us."

I told Addison I had to go and I left her house.

On my way home, I stopped to practice some farts. By that point I had kale 4 times so it was a good time for a test.

**"BBBBBBBRRRRRRRRRZZZZZZZ
ZZZTHHHRRRRRRRPPPPPPPPPPPPP
PPPPPPPPPPPPPPPPPPPPPPPPPPPPPP
PPPPPPPPPPPPPPPPTTTHHHH"**

The kale fart was insane, I almost started a fire!

Friday

When I reached our secret meeting place in the woods, Steve was already there, along with CJ, she's LJ's sister.

"I think you know CJ," Steve said.

"Yes, I do. Hi, CJ."

"Hey. Are you as worried as we are?"

"I am actually more sad than worried. I just can't understand how one of our own people could work against us."

"I know, but at this point we can't afford to be emotional. We have to identify the spy and punish him or her, and we'll have to do it quickly."

CJ was right. I won't be able to do my job and help the mobs in the village if I become too emotional. Now that everyone is looking up to me, I have to be responsible. I gathered my thoughts and said, "First, we have to find out how it's even possible that someone could spy on us without us knowing it."

"I think I know the answer to that mystery," LJ said.

"There are some zombies in the village who wonder around all the time, they're gradually losing all their body parts, so we stay away from them, but it's possible one of the humans talked to them."

"Are they allowed to go everywhere?" I asked.

"Yea. They can go wherever they want."

"That means they have probably seen everything, but have understood very little. I think it's possible that someone innocently mentioned that he has seen a creeper coming to the village."

"You mean the person has not served as a secret agent, but has just answered a simple question without knowing how that will harm his own clan?"

"Exactly!"

"But still, we'll have to confirm that."

"Yes, and we can't waste any time! Training begins tomorrow!"

"We have to plan our approach carefully. We can't just go up to them and ask them direct questions."

CJ broke her silence. "I'll talk to them," she volunteered. "The oldest one among them is my uncle, my dad's brother. I think you guys are right. From everything I know about them, they're not the type who would hurt us on purpose."

"Do you want us to go with you?" Steve asked. "Or would you rather just do the job yourself and meet us here later?"

"You said that you need to meet the Ender today. You should go ahead and take care of that. I'll come back here after a couple of hours."

"What should I do, then? Should I join you, Steve?" I asked.

"I think you should go home and get some rest. Starting tomorrow, you're going to have to work more than any of us. So you deserve to have some lazy time now. I'll call you and give you an update later."

"Okay, you're probably right. I don't think there's anything else I can do here today, so it would be better if I go back home practice some farts. I might even make a training schedule for everyone."

"By the way, did you get a chance to check out the books at the library?"

"Yea, I did. I didn't come across any useful information about relationships between creepers and wolves. But I found out something really important."

"What's that?" CJ asked.

"We have to gather pork chops for managing the wolves."

"What are the pork chops for?"

"We'll put kale inside the pork chops. I read that when someone holds pork chops in front of the wolves, they just stare at them and drool until they can eat it, and they completely forget about the real job."

"What happens if they eat the kale, will they explode?" Steve asked.

"We'll find out. I'll ask my mom to get the pork chops ready for us. She has a bunch of kale at home too."

"Okay. Try to get the recipe from your mom and we can ask the cooks in the village to make extra just in case."

I left and started walking towards my house. Tomorrow I'm going to train the skeletons to fart. I think we can use it against the humans. I read that skeletons can fart from the hole in their eyes, so if the humans look at them they'll get a bunch of fart right in their face! This is going to be awesome!

- End of Book 2 -

Wimpy Fart Books

Book 3 is now available!

Also available on Amazon.com

is a new series:

Diary of Harry Farter

(Harry Potter's Secret Cousin)

Made in the USA
Middletown, DE
12 January 2018